TO A SPECIAL LITTLE BUNNY:

ISBN 979-8-88685-384-1 (paperback)
ISBN 979-8-88685-448-0 (hardcover)
ISBN 979-8-88685-385-8 (digital)

Copyright © 2023 by Kim Timmington

All rights reserved. No part of this publication may be reproduced, distributed, or transmitted in any form or by any means, including photocopying, recording, or other electronic or mechanical methods without the prior written permission of the publisher. For permission requests, solicit the publisher via the address below.

Christian Faith Publishing
832 Park Avenue
Meadville, PA 16335
www.christianfaithpublishing.com

Illustrations by: Sherry and Eric Lee

Printed in the United States of America

I dedicate this book to my husband, Jeff; children, Mae, Sam, Joanna, and Trinity; mom, Paula; sister, Karla; and dear grandma, Carolyn.

—Kim

We dedicate this book to our beloved furbabies, Alfie and Libby.

—Sherry and Eric

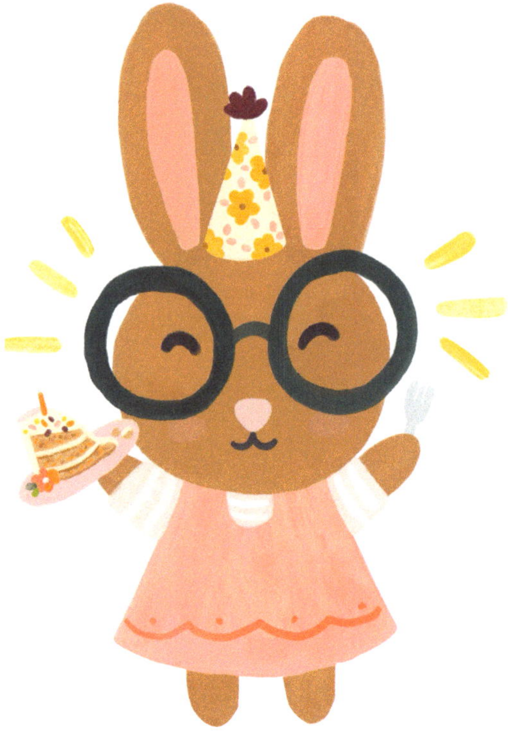

A Bunny's Best Birthday!

Written by
Kim Timmington

Illustrated by
Sherry & Eric Lee

Once upon a time, there was a young bunny named Rue.
Her birthday was coming up, and she didn't know what to do.

She asked her family to help figure out fun plans.
"Do an acorn scavenger hunt at the park!" suggested her sister, Fran.

"Or we could go to the apple orchard and pick apples from the trees. We could stay outside all day long and play with our friends, the bees."

"Granny Smith, Honeycrisp, and McIntosh Red.
We can take our apples home to make delicious pie and bread!"

Rue replied, "But what if it's raining or cold on my birthday? October in Michigan can be so chilly and gray."

"We will stay inside," said Fran, "and do whatever you please."
"We'll make happy memories in the warm where we won't freeze!"

"At home, we can make party hats for our heads!
We'll wear them all day long and paint with the color red."

"We'll also paint with orange, yellow, green, and blue.
Last but not least, beautiful purple too."

"And then we'll hang the piñata up and gather every bunny.
We'll take turns swinging the bat. It will be oh-so-funny!"

"I wonder which one of us will have the best aim."
"I love that," said Rue. "It's the perfect birthday game!"

"What about my birthday cake?" Rue started to ask.
"Thanks for mentioning," said Mom. "It's the very best task!"

"Together, we can make a scrumptious carrot cake.
You'll whisk the ingredients. Then in the oven, it will bake."

"After, we'll whip up a simple cream cheese frosting.
We'll take turns mixing because it's so exhausting."

"We'll frost the cake and decorate it with sprinkles galore.
And top it off with candles and a golden number four."

"We'll put our freshest flowers on the cake's plate.
This cake won't look good… It will look GREAT!"

"Next, pizza for supper, that's an absolute must!
We'll put your favorite toppings on a cauliflower crust."

"Can't forget a salad with tasty kale and beets.
Along with diced yams, so it tastes a little sweet."

"And after that, it's cake time!" Brother Bunny exclaimed.
"We'll sing to you, you'll make a wish, and blow out the flames."

"Everyone will smile and cheer and clap so very loud.
You'll feel on top of the world—so happy, loved, and proud!"

"You'll taste your cake and I know you won't have any words!
You'll have to get a second helping… Maybe even thirds!"

"Finally, we'll end the night by getting on our feet.
We'll turn the music up and dance along to the beat."

"We'll twirl, twist, hop, and dance the night away.
Sounds like the best birthday, wouldn't you say?"

"Yes, absolutely," said Bunny Rue.
"But now after talking and thinking it through…"

"It doesn't matter the weather or what we do.
I'll have the best birthday, as long as I'm with all of you."

"But don't forget the piñata too!"

Printed in the USA
CPSIA information can be obtained
at www.ICGtesting.com
LVHW061706190923
758630LV00007B/232